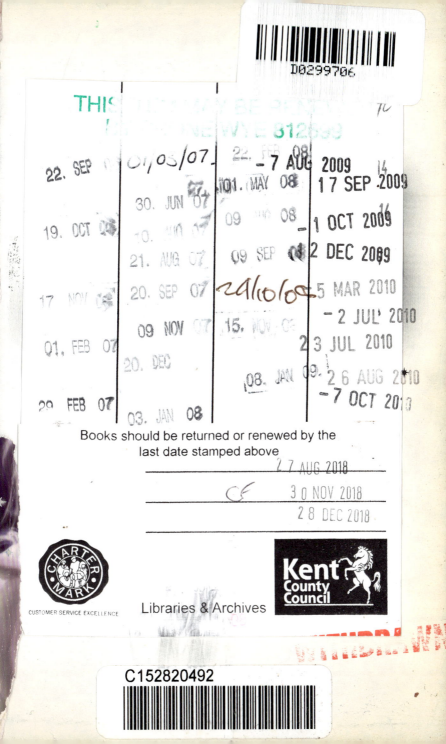

The **My Magical Pony** series:

Other series by Jenny Oldfield:

Pale Moon

By Jenny Oldfield

Illustrated by Gillian Martin

Hodder
Children's
Books

A division of Hodder Headline Limited

Chapter One

"This is wild!" Nathan Steele yelled at Krista as they galloped their ponies along the beach.

Krista crouched low over Drifter's neck like a race jockey. The horse's hooves thundered, his tail streamed behind him. "I'll race you to Black Point!" she cried.

Nathan was riding Shandy, a stocky pony with a big heart. She set her sights on the distant headland and galloped for all she was worth.

Drifter was faster – his long legs covered more ground – so Krista pulled ahead. "Cool!"

Krista sighed. She felt the spray from the waves, heard them crash against the jagged rocks ahead.

"Yee-hah!" Nathan gave a cowboy yell. He tugged on his right rein and swerved Shandy towards the sea. Soon they were galloping through the shallow water.

"Whoa!" At Black Point Krista pulled up her chestnut pony. She glanced over her shoulder to see Nathan and Shandy charging after them in a haze of sparkling droplets, caught in the pale autumn sunlight like a million diamonds. "Wicked!" she grinned, and turned Drifter to face them.

"You win!" Nathan said breathlessly.

"Let's give the ponies a break," Krista

decided, taking her feet out of the stirrups to stretch her legs. She watched the foaming white water swirl amongst the dark rocks and breathed in the sea air. "Are you going to the bonfire party on Saturday?" she asked, knowing that Nathan's family didn't go out into town much.

"Which one?"

"In Whitton, at the football field."

"What time?"

"Seven o'clock. Every year they have a big firework display, plus a guy and everything. It's cool."

"I reckon I might come," Nathan replied, leaning forward to pat Shandy's neck.

The two ponies breathed heavily, their sides heaving in and out. In the chill November air, their warm breath turned into clouds of steam.

"Cool!" Krista nodded, then gently pressed her heels against Drifter's flanks. He eased into a walk back along the beach. "Everyone will be there," she promised.

Pale Moon

"What's your favourite firework?" Nathan asked as he and Shandy came alongside.

Krista thought for a while. "The ones that shoot up different coloured flashes of light that explode into thousands of sparks," she decided, trying to remember the name.

"Roman candles. I like rockets. They go really high."

"I like them too," she agreed. Thinking ahead to Saturday, she knew she would have to do all her chores at Hartfell stables and finish early if she wanted to be in time for the bonfire.

That meant mucking out, cleaning the tack, and putting it away as fast as she could. Then she would have to help Jo Weston,

the stable owner, to feed the ponies. With luck she could be away by half-five.

"… Or the ones that whizz round in a circle," Nathan went on. "Catherine wheels."

"Hmmm. I like them all!" Krista squeezed Drifter's sides again and urged him into a trot.

He picked up his feet and high-stepped through the curving wave that had just broken on the shore.

"Look, Spike – blackberries!" Back home at High Point Farm, Krista crouched down to hedgehog level and jiggled a plastic carton under his nose. "They're the last ones of the season. I'm going to collect a few more so Mum can make a crumble."

Pale Moon

Her pet hedgehog snuffled at the berries.

Krista took one out of the box and offered it to him on her palm. "You'll like them – they taste sweet."

Spike gobbled the juicy blackberry then ambled off towards the hedge at the bottom of the garden.

"Don't go nosing around in any strange bonfires!" Krista called after him anxiously. "They might seem dry and warm to you, but they're dangerous places for a hedgehog to shelter in!"

Spike waddled on without looking back.

Krista sighed. Bonfire Night was good fun, but she did worry about Spike. About all animals, come to think of it. November the fifth was definitely a time for cats and dogs to stay indoors, and for horses to be in their stables, out of harm's way.

"Krista, it's going to rain. Come inside!" her mum shouted from the kitchen doorway.

Krista looked up at the heavy grey sky. She didn't mind getting wet. "Can't I stay

out and collect more blackberries?"

Her mum tutted then gave in. "Just for a few minutes."

"Great, thanks!" Krista ran and overtook Spike, slipping out of the back gate and sprinting down the lane towards the cliff path. She knew a great place for blackberries.

Quickly she climbed the stile, and, without looking down from the path towards the wide curve of Whitton Bay, she sprinted along the narrow track until she came to a high mound of blackberry bushes that straggled over the barbed wire fence and down the slope towards the cliffs. As she'd thought, there was still plenty of fruit left. She reached out and began to pluck the plump berries from their stalks.

13

The box grew full. At this rate there would soon be plenty to make a crumble. "Magic!" Krista murmured. Then she laughed at herself.

Sure, it was cool to be out here picking berries in the drizzling mist, looking down on a windswept bay. But Krista knew something about this place that she shared with nobody, and it was a secret that involved real magic!

Here, on this spot, she had first met Shining Star, her magical pony.

He had appeared in a glittering cloud. Krista had stared in disbelief. A pure white pony had hovered above her, his wings spread wide. He had called her name and said he came from the world of Galishe to help those in trouble.

Pale Moon

That had been the first time and there had
been many since.

Shining Star would appear as a low silver
cloud drifting in from the sea or down from
the horizon of Hartfell Moor. Krista would
hear him whisper her name and she would run

to the magic spot, waiting breathlessly as the cloud broke up into beautiful silver dust which drifted down to the ground to reveal her magical pony.

"Krista, I need you," he would say. She'd climb on his back and they'd fly high into the sky where no one could see them as they passed through days and nights, between worlds.

Now though, there was no sign of Shining Star on the dull grey horizon and Krista happily picked blackberries until her carton was full.

Soon she wiped her stained hands on the wet grass and then stood up. "Hi, Shining Star!" she murmured to the empty sky, just in

16

case he was listening. "If you need me, just call!"

She waited a few moments but there was no reply. All must be well.

Nodding, then firmly fastening the lid on her box, Krista ran home.

"Yum!" Krista's dad sighed, dropping his spoon into his empty dish. "Blackberry crumble and custard – my favourite."

Krista put her hands over her stomach. "I'm full!" she groaned.

Her dad got up from the table. "Come on then. A bit of exercise will do you good."

Krista wasn't so sure. It was dark and the drizzle had turned to heavy rain. "What kind of exercise?"

My Magical Pony

"You remember the low branches I cut from the trees in the back garden the other day? I want to load them on to the trailer and take them down to the bonfire in town."

"Oh, Dad, can't I watch telly?" Krista groaned. Just for once she wanted to veg out, even though she knew there was only one day to go before the big event. "You could take them tomorrow while I'm at the stables."

"I can't," he explained, putting on his jacket. "I have to work tomorrow. It's now or never."

Sighing, Krista stuffed her feet into her

wellies and followed him out into the wet
yard. She helped lift the heavy branches and
tie them safely on to the open trailer. "Rain,
rain, rain!" she moaned. "At this rate they
won't be able to light the bonfire tomorrow."

"These last few days have been pretty wet,"
her dad admitted. "I just heard a flood
warning on the weather forecast." Checking
the knots that held the branches in place, he
jumped in the car and eased out of the yard.

Twenty minutes later they drew up in the
Whitton Football Club car park.

"How's it going, Jim? We've brought more
fuel for the fire!" Krista's dad called to one of
the men standing next to a mountain of wood

19

stacked on the field. The bonfire towered five metres into the air and smelt of old wood, earth and leaves.

Krista helped her dad drag the branches towards the stack, seeing through the gloom that it was made up of old planks, doors, more branches, wooden chairs, even an old sofa that someone had thrown out. As she struggled with her branch, she slipped and almost fell over in the mud.

"Here, let me take that," Jim Kerr offered, lifting it and tossing it high on to the pile.

"It's a bigger fire than last year," Krista said, growing excited now that she was here. "Where's the guy?"

"In the clubhouse, having finishing touches

20

put to him by my two daughters," Jim told her with a grin.

Krista ran to sneak a look, finding two older girls stuffing straw inside the guy's shirt, plonking a tatty blonde wig on his head and drawing a face with felt tip pens. In a corner she spotted a big stack of cardboard boxes. "Are those the fireworks?" she asked.

"He looks like a woman!" Alice Kerr shrieked, ignoring Krista and watching her sister go mad with red marker pen for the lips.

"Who cares?" Amy giggled. "He's going up in smoke anyway!"

Krista grinned. "Cool guy!" she told them, dashing back to join her dad.

"Ready?" he asked.

She took one last look at the dark tower of wood, breathed in the smell of trampled grass and wet leaves, then nodded. "It's going to be great!" she announced.

For once Krista could hardly wait for her day at the stables to be over – so the bonfire fun could begin.

Chapter Two

"More rain!" Krista's mum sighed, listening to the radio over breakfast next morning.

Krista was ready to leave for Hartfell, dressed in a thick red jumper and woollen scarf, her jeans tucked into her wellies.

"A large area of low pressure over the Atlantic is bringing steady rain to all parts," the voice on the radio told them.

"Maybe we'll be lucky in this area," Krista's mum muttered. She turned off the radio and shooed her daughter out into the wet yard.

"The football field is going to be a mud-bath later tonight," she predicted.

Sitting in the car on the way to the stables, Krista stared out at the grey scene, searching the sky for a tiny chink of blue. "Will we still have fireworks if it carries on raining?" she asked.

Her mum tootled down the hill, round sharp bends, windscreen wipers swishing. "I've never known them cancel the football club bonfire in all the years it's been going," she assured Krista. "Did you bring your waterproof jacket?"

"It's in the boot."

The car splashed through a giant puddle into Jo's stable yard then stopped.

24

Pale Moon

Krista jumped out and grabbed her luminous yellow riding jacket. She reminded her mum to pick her up at half past, then ran across the yard into the shelter of the tack room.

Jo's two black cats sat snugly on a pile of horse rugs. Jo herself was sorting out headcollars. "Hi, Krista," she said brightly. "The rain didn't put you off, I see!"

"As if!" Krista helped with the headcollars. "Who shall I muck out first?"

"You can begin with Misty then move on down the row. I'll come and help when I've finished here."

Once more Krista crossed the yard. "Hi, Misty, it's me!" she said, unbolting the little grey pony's door and sliding quickly in.

Misty snickered and came up to nuzzle Krista's sleeve. She was a dainty, dappled mare with gentle brown eyes and a pretty face.

"I don't have any treats," Krista told her with a laugh, getting to work on the bed of straw.

Misty stood by the door, half watching Krista, but with an eye on the outside world.

Soon other cars arrived. First Nathan's dad dropped him off and stopped for a quick chat

with Jo. Then Carrie Jordan and Janey
Bellwood arrived together, followed by Alan
Lewis in his muddy Land Rover with his
young son Will.

"The rain doesn't seem to have dampened
anyone's spirits," Jo commented as she started
mucking out next door. "We'll get Misty,
Comanche, Drifter and Shandy ready first.
Will can ride Shandy today."

Krista worked hard to groom and tack up
the four ponies on Jo's list.

"Who am I riding?" Will pestered, the top
of his blond head hardly reaching the level of
the stable door.

Krista was brushing the dark bay's
broad back. "This one. Her name's Shandy,"

27

she answered, smiling as Will whooped and ran off to tell his dad.

Meanwhile, Nathan was waiting for his lesson with Jo in the arena, so he sauntered across. He watched as Krista carefully placed Shandy's saddle on the pony's back.

Krista and Nathan chatted for a while. "Did you hear, the fireworks are cancelled because of the rain?" he dropped in casually.

"No!" she cried in disgust.

"Only kidding!" he quipped, running off before she could get her own back.

Before too long the ponies were saddled, Nathan was in the arena riding Misty and Krista had chosen the chestnut thoroughbred, Scottie. She was at the head of the small

28

group riding out along the cliff path.

"Don't go near the beach," Jo warned from the arena as Krista led Carrie, Janey and Will out of the yard. "The wind is blowing straight off the sea. It's high tide so the waves will be smashing against the base of the cliffs."

My Magical Pony

So Krista decided on a safe, sheltered bridle track that would usually give them a good view of Whitton Bay.

"Can't see a thing!" Carrie muttered, keeping Misty in check and peering into the gusting rain.

Drops splattered on to their hard hats and rolled over the peaks, their jackets were drenched. It was the sort of rain that got into every nook and cranny.

The ponies plodded on along the narrow track. Their coats were sodden and their manes hung limply against their necks.

On Scottie at the head of the single file, Krista hardly noticed when they passed the magic spot. *Who'd believe there was a beautiful*

beach down there in all that murk? she thought.

Drip-drip-drip. Through the mist and the rain, the four ponies and their riders plodded on.

"Hot soup!" Back in the tack room, Jo offered Krista a warm and filling lunch. "How was the ride this morning?"

"Wet!" Krista smiled. "But good. Will kept telling bad knock-knock jokes and making us laugh even though we were all soaked to the skin."

"Nathan's doing pretty well with his lessons," Jo reported. "He wants to start learning how to jump."

Krista stared out at the puddles.

31

My Magical Pony

There seemed to be fewer drops disturbing their shiny surface. "Hey, the rain's stopping!" she cried. She looked up to see breaks in the cloud and bright patches of blue sky showing through. "Maybe the weather will be OK for the bonfire after all!"

As the rain stopped and the sky brightened, Jo and Krista finished their lunch and got ready for the afternoon rides. This time Jo decided to lead the trek and asked Krista to work with her own horse, Apollo, in the arena.

"Practise some dressage with him," she told Krista. "He doesn't move from trot to canter as smoothly as he should."

Krista was proud to work with the

champion show-jumper. He was a gorgeous grey – sixteen hands high, with long elegant legs and a beautiful sleek head. He responded well to the exercises she set him and she soon had him changing paces brilliantly.

Afterwards, she took him back to his stable

and gave him a special sponge down with lukewarm water mixed with lavender-wash.

Then Jo's group came back and it was time to brush and feed the ponies after a hard day's work. The afternoon had flown by, and by now the clouds had completely lifted, driven away by a fresh breeze.

It was already growing dark as Krista took buckets into all the stables, watching the ponies put their heads down and munch noisily at the mix of oats, molasses and sugar beet. "Here you are, Shandy," she murmured, taking the last bucket into the corner stable.

A bright, red-breasted robin flew out as she went in.

Pale Moon

Shandy ate greedily inside her dark stable, her back turned to Krista.

"Time for you to go!" Jo called as headlights swept across the yard. "Your mum's here!"

At last – time for a bonfire and a firework spectacular! Krista bolted the stable door and said goodbye to Shandy, then sprinted for the car.

Chapter Three

Everyone was in a mad rush at High Point Farm.

Krista's mum made a speedy meal of sausage and mash while her dad had a quick shower. He came down in a dark blue sweatshirt and jeans, his hair still wet.

Meanwhile, Krista dashed out to check on Spike.

"Here, Spike, yummy food!" she called, shining her torch into the hedge bottom. She put down his dish and called again.

Soon he came ambling up the lawn,

a spiky little creature with a black face and beady eyes glinting in the torchlight.

Krista watched him tuck in to his supper. "Now, Spike, I want you to stay in tonight!" she told him sternly. "No wandering off!"

Spike slurped and gobbled.

"There's your nest-box, remember!" Aiming the torch at his little wooden home on the top edge of the lawn, Krista explained why he shouldn't go walkabout. "It's lovely and warm for you, all lined with nice dry leaves. You can snuggle in there while there are all these fires and sparkly things that go fizz and bang, which you won't like, believe me! You can come out tomorrow morning when it's all over and it's safe for you to go wandering again."

37

Spike's dish was soon empty. He sniffed the air then wrinkled his little black nose.

"That's bonfire smoke you can smell," Krista told him. "People are already lighting them all over the place. Nasty for hedgehogs – yuck!"

As if he understood, Spike began to amble up the lawn towards his cosy nest-box. He sniffed at the entrance, dug the soft earth for a while with his sharp claws then disappeared inside.

Pale Moon

"Good boy!" Krista sighed. It was almost time for Spike to hibernate and it was clear that he was feeling pretty sleepy. Satisfied, she switched off her torch and ran back into the house.

"Ready?" her mum asked. She'd packed a bag with a flask of coffee and a tin full of home-made gingerbread. "Your dad's waiting outside in the car."

Krista sat on the back seat, gazing out at the dark, clear night, looking for signs of other, more distant fires. "There's one!" she cried, picking out the spot where a soft red glow lit the horizon. "And there!" She pointed across the moors in the direction of Moorside Farm. "Will said his dad had

built a *hu-uge, humungous* bonfire!"

Her dad wound down the window. "Smell the smoke in the air!" he said, as suddenly the sky behind them exploded in a shower of bright green and red sparks.

"Wow!" Krista said. "Hurry up, Dad. We're going to miss the start!"

They arrived at the field just in time to see Jim Kerr's two daughters carry the guy from the clubhouse. Jim took the stuffed figure from them then climbed a ladder which had been propped against the high bonfire. Carefully he climbed it and placed the guy on top.

"Hi there!" John Steele, Nathan's dad, greeted Krista's mum and dad. "Good to

see that the rain has cleared."

Krista spotted lots of friends, but made a beeline for John Carter, the vet, with his young son, Henry.

"Stand well back!" Jim ordered as he began to light the fire.

The flames spluttered slowly into life, catching at kindling set around the base of the bonfire then licking at the larger planks and branches.

"The wood's pretty wet," Krista's dad commented, watching the slow progress of the yellow flames.

Krista watched impatiently. She wanted to see the fire rise high and watch the red sparks dance in the night sky.

Gradually the fire took hold. The burning wood crackled and hissed. A dense smoke rose.

"Cool smell!" Carrie said, breathing in the wood smoke.

"Look at the guy!" Nathan stood breathless as the scarecrow figure was quickly swallowed by flames.

"Remember, remember the fifth of November, gunpowder, treason and plot!" Krista's dad chanted. "I see no reason why gunpowder treason should ever be forgot!"

Whoosh! Guy Fawkes was gone!

A shiver ran down Krista's spine in spite of the heat from the fire.

Then the fireworks started and she forgot

43

all about traitors. She heard the whoosh of
rockets and Roman candles and watched them
blossom into huge flower shapes above their
heads, slowly fading as they drifted to earth.

"Golden Willow!" Jim announced, as a
firework sent golden arches high into the
darkness. They divided into a hundred
branches that crackled and sparkled.

Spring fountains, silver spinners, screaming
serpents – fireworks whizzed and burst, filling
the sky with bright colour. Catherine wheels
whirled gracefully, thunderbolts rattled like
heavy gunfire.

"Wow!" Krista said over and over, her
neck aching from tilting her head back. She
seemed to have been smiling non-stop since

44

the start of the display. "Does Henry like the fireworks?" she asked John Carter, who was still standing next to her holding the toddler.

"He loves 'em," the vet grinned.

Henry reached out both arms as if trying to catch the twinkling lights. In the glow of the bonfire his round cheeks looked rosy, his eyes shone with delight.

All too soon though, the fireworks ended in a spectacular burst of fan-shaped golden sparks and silver comets splitting into shoals of tiny, wriggling fish-like creatures that faded before they hit the earth.

"That's it!" Jim told them.

"Aaaah!" There was a general sigh of disappointment, then a loud burst of applause.

"Brilliant!" the grown-ups said. "The best ever."

The kids said nothing, their mouths already stuffed full of gingerbread or treacle toffee.

Remember, remember, the fifth of November … Krista thought. How could anyone forget the bright lights, the flames, the bangs? Her face tingled from the heat of the fire, her ears hummed.

As the fire began to die down and the ashes settled, she turned to stare up at the moors, which lay in black shadow. By now most of the fires on the hillside were out and the fireworks over, except for an occasional rocket shooting like a comet into the sky.

Pale Moon

Krista sighed. She was about to turn back
to the bonfire when a wispy cloud on the
horizon caught her attention.

That's weird, she thought, and looked again.

The lonely cloud was definitely there.
It was small, floating over the top of the hill
and drifting slowly down the moorside.

"It's silver!" Krista murmured out loud.

"Krista, would you like more gingerbread?" her mum called.

Krista shook her head. Where had the cloud gone now? Searching the dark hillside, she spotted it again – wispy and faint, shedding a mist of sparkling droplets on to the moor.

Shining Star! Krista was certain it was her magical pony. He was waiting for her to come!

But how could she leave the bonfire party and get to him in the darkness?

He needs you! she told herself firmly.

"I can't get away," she muttered back.

Someone needs help!

"I know! What do you expect me to do?"

"Talking to yourself again?" her dad asked
as he passed by holding a mug of coffee.
He reached out and ruffled her hair.

"Dad, don't do that!" she pleaded.

How long would Shining Star wait? She looked
anxiously up the hillside. "Can we go now?"
she asked.

Her dad grinned. "What's the rush? Hold
your horses! Ha – good joke! Horses!"

"It's not funny, Dad! I'm – er – tired. I need
to go to bed."

The small silver cloud was still there.
Shining Star was definitely waiting for her at
the magic spot.

"Well, blow me down!" her dad muttered,

49

gulping his coffee and going off to tell her
mum. "Ruth, Krista can't be feeling well. She
says she wants to go home!"

"Are you sure you're OK?" Krista's mum felt
Krista's forehead to check her temperature.

They'd got home early from the bonfire,
back to their cosy farmhouse on the hill.
Now her mum and dad were sure she must
be ill.

"I'm fine – just tired," Krista insisted. She
was longing to race upstairs and look out of
her window to see if the wispy silver cloud
was still there.

"Here are your pyjamas," her dad said,
bringing them into the kitchen and putting

them by the fireside. "Get changed where it's warm."

"I'm OK, honest!" Krista wished they would stop fussing. She needed to be alone.

Shining Star won't wait much longer! she told herself.

"Have a drink of hot chocolate," her mum suggested.

"No thanks."

Her mum and dad frowned at one another. "She's definitely not herself," her dad said.

Quickly Krista slipped into her pyjamas. "I'm off to bed. Good night!"

Before they could stop her, she shot out of the room and took the stairs two at a time. She flung open her bedroom door and dashed to the window.

Shining Star, here I am! Leaning out into the cold night air, she tried to let her magical pony know that she'd come to answer his call at last.

The night had fallen silent. The last fireworks had faded from the sky.

I'm here! Desperately Krista longed to see

Pale Moon

the magic cloud drift across the moor from the magic spot. *It's hard for me to sneak out, Shining Star. You'll have to come and find me!*

But there was no movement on the hillside – no sparkling cloud, no beautiful white pony emerging from the silver mist.

"I'm too late!" Krista murmured sadly.

She waited and waited, but her magical pony didn't come.

Chapter Four

Sadly Krista went to bed and crawled under the duvet.

I'm sure it was Shining Star! she thought.

But she hadn't been able to get away to meet him at the magic spot, and now she felt certain that she'd let him down.

"Sorry!" she whispered, her head turned towards the window. She saw the moon low over the horizon, but no clouds in the sky.

For a while Krista lay wondering why Shining Star had come to find her and what kind of help he needed. She imagined

climbing on his back and rising from the ground, flying over rooftops to a distant town, or even as far as the stars. *Someone somewhere needs us!* she sighed to herself.

Soon though, the comfort of her warm bed settled her thoughts. Her eyelids closed and she began to drift off to sleep.

In her dream she saw bright fireworks. She was in an aeroplane, flying above bonfires, in amongst the exploding sparks. Out of the window she saw a comet speed past, trailing a tail of golden light.

"Krista!" a voice called.

The dream plane rose through a bank of white clouds until it was close to a pale, full moon. She could see a glow of silver light.

My Magical Pony

"Krista, wake up!"

The plane lurched sideways. Krista
jerked awake. She was in her bedroom. The
window was open and a bright cloud hung
low in the sky.

"At last!" Shining Star said.

A breeze blew the silver cloud closer to
the house until it almost seemed to enter
through the window.

Krista slid out of bed. The night air was
cold and damp as she leaned out to touch the
sparkling dust.

A few moments later, as the dust fell
to the ground, the magical pony appeared.
Krista made out his beautiful white head
and long mane, his dark, wise eyes.

Then, beating his wings slowly, he dropped gently on to the grass and gazed up at her.

"What's happened?" Krista whispered, afraid that she might wake her mum and dad. "Why have you come?"

My Magical Pony

The magical pony kept his wings spread wide. Silvery moonlight fell on his broad white back. "There is danger," he said quietly. "It is very grave."

"Where? Is it nearby?"

"No, it is far from here," the pony told her. "In another town beside another sea, where a river runs." As he spoke, he quivered and breathed silver mist into the air.

Krista heard a fear in her magical pony's voice that she had never heard before. "And who needs help?"

"There were ponies trapped by rising water," Shining Star explained. "The river ran fast and dangerous into the sea."

"Have the ponies been saved?" Krista cried,

almost forgetting to keep her voice down.

"Not yet," he replied. "Rain beats down on them, the river rises."

"Oh, that's awful!" Krista felt panic rise inside her, like the flood water he talked of.

"Wait. You have not heard all," Shining Star insisted. "A message came to the land of Galishe that the creatures would drown without our help. My sister, Pale Moon, was chosen to fly there and see what could be done."

Krista nodded. She held her breath, dreading what was coming next.

"Pale Moon flew through the heavens to earth, above a thousand fires, through a strange sky full of shooting sparks of many colours."

"It was Bonfire Night," Krista explained.

"People let off fireworks. Did she find the ponies?"

Shining Star nodded. "They were huddled on a dark hillside, trapped on one side by sheer rock, on another by the raging river, and on the third side by the wild sea. The rain fell in torrents, the wind blew savagely. Pale Moon looked down and saw that there was a way to safety, if only she could lead the ponies down the hill towards an old stone bridge that would take them to dry land."

"And did she?"

The magical pony took a deep breath. "Pale Moon landed and began to lead the group towards the bridge. All this we could see from Galishe. But we could not warn her."

Pale Moon

Krista heard Star falter. "Warn her about what?"

"The river raged towards the sea," Star went on. "As Pale Moon set foot on the bridge, with the frightened  ponies huddled behind her, a great wave of black water swept down the hillside and crashed into it, smashing the stones that supported the bridge. The ponies who followed my sister saw that the structure

would tumble into the wave and so they ran
back the way they had come."

"But what happened to Pale Moon?" Krista
whispered.

Shining Star looked up, his voice trembling.
"She could not turn back. The stones of the
bridge collapsed under her and she fell into
the dark wave."

"And then what?" Krista gasped. She
couldn't believe that one of the wonderful
magical ponies of Galishe was dead.

But Star shook his head in despair. "We
do not know," he confessed. "The bridge
vanished, taking my sister with it. Come,
Krista, leave your bed. We must make haste
to find her!"

Chapter Five

Krista didn't hesitate. Swiftly getting dressed, she went back to the window and whispered to Shining Star that she would join him in the garden.

Quietly she turned the door handle and crept out of her room, along the landing past her mum and dad's bedroom, down the stairs. In the kitchen the embers of the fire still glowed.

Krista put on her boots then paused for breath. Her chest felt tight with worry as she slipped out of the back door into the moonlight.

My Magical Pony

"Make haste," Shining Star urged, standing with his wings spread wide, surrounded by his glittering silver cloud.

Krista looked swiftly over her shoulder at the quiet house then ran to him. She scrambled on to his back, tucking her legs behind the powerful wings and taking hold of his white mane.

The magical pony beat his wings and steadily rose from the ground.

Krista looked down. It was strange to see her home from above – the grey roof, the cobbled yard and the smooth green lawn. A wisp of smoke still rose from the chimney.

"Hold tight," Star told her.

He surged upwards, over Hartfell, higher

than the highest cliffs on the wild moor top.

Krista could only just make out the rough dark boulders before they sped on, inland towards the small villages scattered across the moor, and on again across a river, over long winding roads lit by streetlamps, over towns and a great city whose orange glow filled the sky.

My Magical Pony

Krista crouched low on Shining Star's back, feeling the wind rush by. Everywhere there was the smell of wood smoke and the glowing remains of bonfires, but now they flew so fast that the world became a blur and she couldn't make out the towns and the hills below.

They were flying faster than any plane, more speedily than the rockets that had so recently lit up the sky. Krista held her breath in wonder.

Before long they flew out of the clear sky into a fierce storm. Rain clouds buffeted them and winds blew them off course.

Shining Star fought the blasts of freezing cold air. He beat his wings strongly, soaring

above the air currents, through the clouds
until they were clear of the storm. He sped
on, heading northwards, his long mane
streaming back into Krista's face, forging his
way through the night sky.

Then, when he judged the time was right,
he plummeted back through the band of dark
cloud to see the land below. Rain beat against
them, soaking them through and blinding
them as they dropped towards the earth.

Krista gasped and held on fast. She saw
dark hills below and heard the wind howl
through trees. Branches creaked and snapped;
the rain poured.

"Are we there?" Krista asked the magical
pony. The dark storm frightened her.

She wished they could land and take stock of what they had to do next.

"This is the place called Thrushcross," Star replied. He swooped over a small town by the sea, whose streets were running with flood water. There was no sign of life, only abandoned cars turned over by the force of the flood, crashed against the corners of empty houses, and uprooted trees blocking the road.

"Where are the people?" Krista wanted to know. The eerie blackness made her skin creep.

"They have been taken to safety in boats and helicopters," Shining Star explained, hovering over what must once have been the

main street of Thrushcross. "The water came
before nightfall, so the people
were able to escape."

Krista gazed down at
the ruined houses. "It's
awful!" she sighed. Water
swirled everywhere,
washing against walls, down
alleyways and through windows into
people's homes. "Show me the bridge where
Pale Moon disappeared."

Shining Star flew over the surging flood,
upstream towards the top of the town.
Here the destruction was worse – houses
had almost disappeared below the flood,
leaving only their roofs above water.

My Magical Pony

Shop signs and doors wrenched off their hinges floated against upturned trees that had smashed what remained in the street.

"The bridge stood by those trees," Shining Star told Krista, making his way towards the spot. "It crossed the river here, where the houses end."

Krista had to peer through the storm. It was very dark and she could scarcely make out objects in the black chaos below. But at last she picked out a ruined stone arch that straddled what had once been the river but was now a swollen torrent.

"My sister, Pale Moon, had led the trapped ponies to this point," Star reminded her. "They fled back on to the hill to the east and

as far as I know, they are still there."

Krista gazed into the darkness but could see nothing. "Is the water still rising?" she asked.

"Until the rain stops the waters will rise," he confirmed. A strong gust of wind blew him closer to the trees that had come crashing down in the storm.

Krista slipped sideways but caught hold of Star's mane just in time. She steadied herself. "And what about Pale Moon?"

"Gone," Star replied. "She was swept from the broken bridge and for a time her head stayed above the water. It took her down through the town, whirling her here and there, crashing her against branches that

71

floated beside her. It pushed her under the surface at last."

"She went under the water?" Krista gasped, hanging on as Shining Star turned and fought the wind to fly back downstream. A wild force of nature battled against him, but he made his slow way towards the river mouth and the open sea.

"Twice Pale Moon vanished below the flood," Star told her. "Twice she fought back to the surface. The flood was swift. It carried her on until she disappeared for a third time."

"And never came back up?" Krista murmured. This was even worse than she'd pictured when Shining Star had first explained the danger his sister was in. She

looked down with fear at the black danger of the raging water.

"We did not see her after her head disappeared for the third time," he said, flying out beyond the mouth of the river towards the sea. Here too there was wreckage from the storm – cars half submerged and trapped in the tiny harbour, small boats tugged from their moorings and smashed against the jetties.

Losing strength after his hard journey, Shining Star flew inland again and sought shelter from the wind between two tall houses overlooking the harbour. He landed carefully on a flat roof and let Krista slide from his back.

73

She stared out at the sheet of rain, feeling hopeless. "Perhaps Pale Moon did drown."

Shining Star folded his wings and stood silently.

"Can ...? Do ...?" Krista tried hard to frame the question that troubled her.

"... Do magical ponies actually die?"

She thought and hoped that perhaps their magic was so strong that nothing ever defeated them and they lived for ever.

"Yes," Star said sadly. "Our lives end just as yours do."

Krista hung her head. "And what happens then?" Surely something – not just nothing! It couldn't be that one minute they were there, surrounded by their wonderful silver mist, doing magic deeds, then suddenly they were no more.

"As we approach the end of life, our shimmering light fades," Shining Star went on. "The light grows dimmer until at last it goes out and our spirits depart."

Star's words made Krista want to cry.

"Where to?" she asked.

"They depart to a silent place among the stars where they may rest for ever. It is called Argennes, a place of peace."

"And might Pale Moon be there?" Krista asked, fighting back her tears. She shivered from head to foot in the cold rain.

"Perhaps," Star murmured. "If she is dead, Argennes will be her final home."

They stood in silence for a while. Krista felt helpless and lost. At their feet the flood water steadily rose.

"I know what we must do," Shining Star said at last, lowering his head and bringing it close to Krista's cold, wet face. "Do you have the courage to make another journey?"

Pale Moon

She gazed into his eyes. "Is it long?"

"Long and far." The magical pony's voice was calm. "We must travel through time and space, to a place you would never think to visit. There we will discover for ourselves if my sister was truly drowned."

Krista nodded. At this moment she would do anything to get away from the cruel storm. "I understand," she told him.

"Do you? Will you come with me to Argennes?"

There was only one doubt in her mind. "What about the ponies on the hill?"

"We will return," Star promised. "When the dawn comes we will help them to escape."

"And it won't be too late?" Krista trusted

Shining Star's wisdom, now as always.

"No one can say for certain how long the storm will last nor how much the waters will rise," he replied honestly. "But before we save the ponies, I must discover what has happened to Pale Moon."

Krista nodded. "I agree," she said quietly.

"Then climb on my back," he urged. "I will take you faraway to the land of the spirits, and bring you back to earth before the sun rises over the sea."

Chapter Six

Shining Star rose from the dark roof overlooking Thrushcross.

Krista flew with him, through a cloud
of silver which began to swirl around them.
It formed a bright tunnel through which Star
sped faster than light.

They were surrounded by a glittering haze,
breathing in the magical dust until they came
to the end of the mysterious tunnel and
entered a sky dotted with twinkling stars and
glowing planets.

Everywhere was silent. The roaring wind

had dropped away and they seemed to float past objects in dark space. Krista saw two flaming meteors ahead of them – molten boulders that crossed their path, leaving behind showers of red-hot sparks. To her left she saw a distant pale green planet spinning slowly on its axis, surrounded by a band of dark green gas. Beneath her, an orange star glowed and gave off heat that she could feel from a great distance.

Shining Star flew on, his wings beating up and down, his white feathers smooth and unruffled.

Krista smiled to herself. The heavens were beautiful, and much more exciting than any firework display back on earth.

Pale Moon

Earth – home! With a shock Krista remembered her friends' faces around the bonfire – little Henry's sparkling eyes and warm cheeks, Nathan's mouth stuffed with toffee, her dad with his mug of coffee. Suddenly she was aware of where she was and what was happening to her, and how special it was to have been singled out by her magical pony.

If Mum and Dad could see me now! she thought, *sailing through the sky, with planets of all colours on every side and stars shining on for ever!*

The magical pony flew straight and sure until he came to a shimmering pale blue star which he circled and then approached.

My Magical Pony

Krista looked down. The star was
surrounded by a haze which they had to pass
through before she saw silvery rock beneath.
She felt the magical pony's hooves touch
down and waited to hear what he had to say.

Pale Moon

"This is our journey's end," he told her, inviting her to step down on to the ground.

Krista did as he asked, gazing around Argennes in wonder.

There were trees growing between the rocks and streams criss-crossing the hillside, but every object and every growing thing glowed silver!

"It's beautiful!" she gasped. It made her think of Christmas and fairy tales. Slowly she walked towards one of the streams and dipped her hand into the brilliant, shining liquid. The ripples spread like molten metal, but the stream was cold to the touch.

Shining Star looked all around. Surrounded by magic mist, he shone brighter than ever, breathing life into this place of the spirits.

"Where is everyone?" Krista asked him. She gazed up at the silver leaves in the trees and down at her feet, where tiny silver flowers grew.

Star nodded towards a nearby hill. On the ridge there was a small group of silent creatures, all ghostly white. Krista saw a young deer, a fox and a stag with great antlers, all grouped together, staring back at them. Beside them stood two white horses.

She gasped and glanced at Shining Star. Could one of these horses be his sister, Pale Moon?

Star stepped slowly towards the spirit creatures and Krista followed him. In the distance she could see more spirits – a lion

84

and her cubs, and a small herd of antelopes, walking together. A great elk with heavy head and massive antlers stood with a wolf who stared calmly at the strangers.

For a moment Krista was afraid. Surely the wolf would attack Shining Star as he approached? He would crouch, then snarl and pounce when they came near. He would bare his fangs and there would be a terrible fight.

But the magical pony walked on and Krista stayed by his side. The white wolf let them pass.

Soon they came to the two horses. The creatures lifted their heads and pricked their ears, alert but unafraid. Star gazed at them for a long time.

85

My Magical Pony

Krista stared. The horses seemed like statues made of marble, so bright and smooth. Their manes flowed like silk over their proud necks, but their eyes, which should have been dark and glistening, were pure white. She gasped and hung back behind Shining Star.

One of the horses stepped forward and addressed them. "Welcome to Argennes," he said softly. "You are Shining Star, from Galishe, are you not? I am Mistral, leader of the horses of Argennes."

Krista stared into the spirit's eyes.

"I seek my sister, Pale Moon," Star replied.

Pale Moon

He glanced at the beautiful spirit horse standing beside Mistral and knew that it was not her.

The deer came close to Krista and stepped daintily around her. The fox padded silently away.

"Her journey to the spirit world has begun," Mistral told Shining Star, "but she has not yet arrived in Argennes."

Krista whispered urgently in Star's ear. "Does that mean she's still alive?"

He nodded.

"We are waiting for her," Mistral went on.

"She is in a place of danger and is fighting to survive. However, without help, she may not succeed."

Still alive! The words echoed inside Krista's head. *We must hurry!* she thought, anxious for Shining Star to find out all he could and then depart.

"So there is little time," Shining Star confirmed. He hesitated then said, "I thank you, Mistral. I know that if my beloved sister loses her fight on earth and it is her destiny to join you here in Argennes, then you will greet her kindly."

The spirit horse nodded. "She will find peace here," he promised. "All creatures will be her friend."

Pale Moon

Standing at Shining Star's side, Krista was amazed to see a clear, shining tear form in the corner of his eye.

With thanks, her magical pony turned away from Mistral. "We hope to keep Pale Moon a while longer in Galishe," he said softly, inviting Krista to mount on to his back. "She is dear to us."

"Then I join you in your hope," the calm spirit horse added.

The deer stood back, beside the

horse and the stag. They watched Krista
climb on Shining Star's back and saw him
spread his wings.

"Pale Moon is alive!" Krista whispered,
close to Star's ear.

"We will find her!" he promised, rising in a
cloud of silver mist, leaving the bright planet
of peaceful spirits to return to the cruel storm
of Krista's world.

Though they had flown through the
wide universe, Krista and Shining Star
arrived back in Thrushcross before dawn.
They found that the rain had stopped at
last and the wind no longer blasted in from
the sea.

Pale Moon

Krista marvelled at the magic that had taken them to Argennes and back before the sun had risen. But there was no time to waste.

Mistral had warned them that Pale Moon was in great danger, so every second lost in searching for her could make all the difference.

"We know that my sister was swept from the bridge when it collapsed," Star said, hovering over the flood water at the top of the town. "The current took her downstream, past the houses, where the water swirled and sucked her down into its depths."

Krista shuddered, but she forced herself to concentrate. "In the end, the water would flow into the harbour," she pointed out. Looking down on the wrecked town –

roofs torn off, upturned cars and vans smashed against walls, flood water still running deep and swift – she noticed the eerie silence. There were no human voices crying for help, no engine sounds, only the water lapping at the buildings and flowing on towards the sea.

Star agreed and turned towards the harbour. He flew slowly above the wreckage, dipping as low as he dared, so that Krista could search for any sign of Pale Moon in the grey dawn light.

She looked anxiously along the street and down alleyways, dreading the sights that might greet her. "Nothing!" she whispered to Star at every bend and corner, half relieved,

but with her hopes of finding his sister alive
rapidly fading.

Soon they came to the last houses in the
town. There was a row of cottages lining the
waterfront, almost submerged beneath the
flood. They overlooked a small harbour,
once full of bright fishing boats and smart
yachts, now littered with the after-effects of
the storm.

"This is terrible!" Krista murmured as she
made out a blue and white boat turned upside
down and crashing against the harbour wall,
beside a huge sheet of rusty metal that looked
as if it had once been part of a workshop
roof. Further on there was the sleek hull of
a sailing boat smashed up against a jetty,

its pointed prow sticking out of the water, its mast jammed against another half-sunk vessel.

As the sky gradually lightened, Krista and Shining Star saw more reasons to be afraid. The flood had carried heaps of smaller objects into the harbour – some still floating, others swamped and half hidden. There were chairs and tables bobbing on the waves, bikes rammed up against boat wreckage, a TV washed on to the deck of a yacht and trapped against the cabin. Worse still, some of the smaller objects were floating free of the harbour, out through a narrow opening between two stone jetties, into the open sea.

"The tide is ebbing," Shining Star noted.

Pale Moon

"Anything that is not moored to the jetties will soon be dragged out to sea."

Krista knew he was right. "If that happens to Pale Moon, we'll never find her!" she gasped.

Her magical pony flew slowly over the harbour, his wings scarcely beating. A pink glow had appeared in the east, but instead of hope, there seemed to be nothing but despair.

My Magical Pony

Then a sound broke the calm that had
descended after the storm. It was the sharp,
frightened bark of a dog – unmistakable, even
though it was muffled and at first there was
no creature to be seen.

"Listen!" Krista said to Star. "I think it's
coming from one of the boats!"

The magical pony hovered close to where
the noise came from. Krista peered down on
the floating wreckage, seeing a smashed hull,
then another half-capsized boat. The barking
grew louder and more desperate. Krista
looked harder still, grasping tight to Shining
Star's mane.

"There!" She pointed to the small cabin
of a blue boat that was turned on its side.

Pale Moon

She saw movement inside, then the face of a terrified grey and black dog.

Shining Star steadied himself about two metres above the water, the tips of his wings almost touching the surface.

"The poor thing is trapped!" Krista gasped. She saw water inside the cabin and realised that it wouldn't be long before the damaged boat sank completely. "We have to rescue it!"

Shining Star nodded. He glanced out to sea, yearning for his lost sister, but he knew they must save the dog's life.

He looked back towards Krista. "This is a hard and dangerous task," he warned. "You must take great care!"

Chapter Seven

How could Krista rescue the dog if there was nowhere for Shining Star to land?

She held tight to Star, trying to work out a way. Over her head a pair of grey seagulls swooped then sailed off on the light breeze. Below, the bedraggled grey and black spaniel yelped and barked at the misted cabin window. His face would appear then disappear as the swell of the sea tossed the slowly sinking boat up and down.

"Can you fly any lower?" Krista asked Shining Star, who shook his head.

Pale Moon

"OK, is there any way I can dismount, stand on the top of the cabin and still hold on to you?"

"Perhaps," he said quietly. "Catch hold of my mane as you lower yourself. I will hold steady, but you must not let go!"

Taking a deep breath and watching in fear as the boat turned and rocked in the water, Krista carefully dismounted. She waited until she could land on the cabin roof, then gently eased herself down.

"Keep hold!" Star said again.

She wound her hand into his long mane, keeping her balance with the other arm. Her feet slipped on the wet, smooth surface, but she soon righted herself and crouched

as low as she could. Through the window, the dog scrabbled at the glass with his front paws.

"OK," she told him, "I've got to find a way to get you out."

She looked for a door in the battered cabin, found one at the back that was meant to slide open and tried it. "It's jammed!" she told Star as a strong wave tossed the boat. "There's nothing else for it – I'll have to break the window!"

He held steady, his great wings beating over her. "Take hold of something heavy," he ordered. "Use it to break the glass."

Pale Moon

Krista felt the force of another wave as it broke against her legs. Still clinging to the pony, she stretched out to one side and found a thick piece of driftwood within reach. Seizing it, she dragged it clear of the salt water and used it like a hammer against the window.

Inside the cabin, the spaniel cowered low. Krista could hear him whimpering.

Once more she raised the heavy stick and hit the glass. It cracked. Slivers slid to the floor, leaving a huge gap.

"Well done," Shining Star said. "But make haste before the waves flood the boat."

Quickly Krista leaned through the window, afraid that she might cut herself,

willing the trapped dog to scramble off the floor to reach her. "Come on, boy, you have to help yourself!"

He understood what he had to do. She felt his tongue lick her fingers and soon slipped her hand through his collar, straining to lift him out of the boat. "Good boy!" she said, praying that she could take his weight and still hold tight to Star's mane.

Soaked by sea spray, straining every muscle, slowly she lifted the dog. He hung limply in her grasp. Krista heaved him through the broken window, clear of the cabin. With a last effort she raised him high and slung him across Shining Star's wide back.

Pale Moon

Under her feet the boat rocked. Water filled the cabin and covered the roof. Quickly she jumped clear and vaulted on to Shining Star. The pony beat his wings and rose above the water.

They flew to safety.

"His name's Ben!" Krista held the dog firmly as Shining Star flew towards land. She read the disc hanging from his collar. "It's OK, boy, you'll be fine!" she whispered.

The dog lay panting in front of her. Water dripped from his tangled fur.

"There is only one place where it is safe for us to land," Star decided, heading for the hill behind flooded Thrushcross town.

My Magical Pony

By now the sun had risen clear above
the sea's flat horizon and was casting long
shadows on the green hill. Trees grew on the
summit, and it was here that the magical pony
was heading.

"As soon as we've dropped Ben off and
checked he's OK, we'll carry on looking for
Pale Moon," Krista
told him.

Pale Moon

"Later, when the flood goes away, we'll find Ben's owner."

Shining Star drew close to the top of the hill and chose a place to land. Exhausted, he dropped to the ground and let his passengers dismount.

Krista laid the dog on the wet grass, noticing that the muddy flood water was only a few metres away. She glanced up to the bare beech trees on the summit. "Look!" she gasped, seeing for the first time the group of wild ponies sheltering under the low branches.

"I had almost forgotten them," Star admitted, folding his wings and stepping out towards the ponies.

My Magical Pony

Staying with Ben, Krista leaned over him and stroked his wet fur. "Everything's going to be OK now," she soothed.

The dog lifted his head to lick her hand, then raised himself from his side and sat quietly.

She stroked him again. "There's no way off the hill until the flood goes down," she said gently, more to herself than to Ben. "You'll have to stay here with the ponies."

The dog stood up and shook himself. He licked her hand again then trotted up the hill after Shining Star.

Krista followed him. She entered the shade of the trees to find her magical pony walking amongst the forlorn herd as if listening and thinking hard.

Pale Moon

The ponies jostled together as she approached. They were small, stocky creatures with thick winter coats and wet, shaggy manes, their heads hanging low, their eyes dull.

"They have given up hope," Star explained to Krista. "The water still rises. Soon they will drown."

She frowned and shook her head. "There must be some way out of here! What's behind these trees?" She ran to the top of the hill and looked down into the next valley. It was only then that she realised what danger the ponies were in, for the land fell away sharply into a sheer drop, impossible for them to climb down. Krista glanced back at Shining Star.

My Magical Pony

"I see why Pale Moon thought that the bridge was the only way to save them!" she gasped. "What do we do now?"

The magical pony shook his head. As the wild ponies shivered under the trees and the flood slowly rose, it was Ben who ran here and there, sniffing at the ground, seeking a way out.

Krista watched the dog run to the very edge of the crag. He peered down, thinking it was a dead-end. But he didn't give in. Instead, he ran back to Krista, barked and ran under the trees, crouched and barked again.

"He wants us to follow," Krista told Star. "He must know the countryside around here pretty well, and it looks like he's got an idea."

Pale Moon

So Shining Star and Krista followed the dog, ducking under low branches until they came up against a tall rock.

"Yes, a dead-end," Krista sighed, surprised when Ben disappeared around the far end of the rocky outcrop. She followed, picking her way over boulders and listening to his excited bark.

He came back into sight, crouching and urging her on.

"Maybe we can bring the ponies this way, down the side of the crag," she muttered. "The flood water hasn't risen this far and it's not such a sheer drop."

Shining Star nodded and went back to fetch the bedraggled herd, while Krista and

109

My Magical Pony

Ben pressed on through rocks and bracken, slowly working their way from the hilltop down a steep, rocky slope. "Yes, I think they'll be able to make it! You're a good boy, Ben. Well done!"

Looking ahead, Krista saw that the hillside was steep and rocky. She glanced back to see

Pale Moon

Shining Star leading the wild ponies into sight. "Tell them to follow us!" she yelled.

Star urged the ponies forward, beyond the rocky outcrop. He edged them down the slope after Krista and Ben.

The ponies slid on the loose stones and mud, putting one foot slowly after another, sometimes slipping against rocks and all trembling as they went. The sun cast long shadows against the hillside, making it hard for Krista to see where she was treading.

"Ouch!" Suddenly her foot was caught in a tangle of barbed wire. She staggered then pulled herself upright. The spikes of the wire had dug into her boot. One had scratched her ankle. "Stop!" she yelled back at Star.

111

Ben crouched and yapped beside her.

"Stay away!" she warned him, stooping to untwist the coil of rusty wire. It was attached to a rotten fence post which she lifted clear of the ground. "OK!" she called to Star and the ponies.

"We'd never have done this in the dark!" Krista muttered as the wild ponies and Shining Star stumbled by. Then she put down the sharp wire and followed the group until Ben reached a flat ledge covered in bracken where the small herd could rest.

Krista looked down into the new valley. There was no flood, and only one or two farmhouses nestling on the low slopes. "Shall we leave them here?" she asked Star.

Pale Moon

He nodded. "The dog will stay with them. We must hurry now." Looking up at the sky, Shining Star told Krista to climb on to his back. "The sun is up," he murmured, "and my sister fights for life."

Krista crouched forward on the magical pony's back. He spread his wings and rose from the rocky ledge. The wind caught his mane and blew it softly against her face. A sob caught in her throat as she pictured the brave white pony battling in the salt water of the harbour, perhaps dragged down and out to sea by the strong pull of the tide. "Where do we start?" she gasped, feeling small and helpless.

Shining Star turned to face the low sun.

He beat his wings steadily, catching the rays so that his body gave off a soft pink glow. Silver mist fell to the ground where the wild ponies stood.

"We start with hope in our hearts," the magical pony replied.

Krista nodded. "Yes. Pale Moon isn't dead!" she said firmly. "Mistral told us that she is putting up a fight."

Star beat his wings more strongly. Below them, the ponies and dog looked up in wonder.

"My sister is brave and clever," Shining Star told Krista. "Though the waters are strong and the sea is wide, we will find her!"

Chapter Eight

The air was calm as Shining Star and Krista flew back over the hill. The storm that had wrecked the little town of Thrushcross had swept out to sea, leaving a strange peace behind.

From high above Krista glimpsed the upturned cars, saw the muddy surge of the river still pouring down the narrow main street, and was glad that she and Star had been able to move the wild ponies out of danger. After all, that had been Pale Moon's mission when she'd first set out from Galishe,

and she would be glad to hear the good news when eventually they discovered her.

If we find her in time! Krista said to herself. The task was hard, but Shining Star had said they must search with hope in their hearts.

Yes, we will find her! Krista insisted. She peered down at the harbour, then out to the glittering sea, longing for a sighting of her magical pony's brave sister.

"Wait!" she whispered. "Look down there!" She'd seen movement near the jetty – a flash of white against the dark stone.

Star swooped lower until they could make out the loose, flapping sail of a wrecked boat, then, disappointed, he rose again into the sky. They flew on, noticing small motor boats

heading towards
the harbour,
coming to survey
the effects of the
storm and begin
the clear-up.

Krista saw gulls circle the
boats, then use air currents to soar into
the blue sky, their grey wings outstretched,
their white breasts flashing in the sun.
They passed by, close enough for her to see
their black, beady eyes and bright orange
beaks, sharp as claws. Her stomach flipped
and she held tight to Star's mane as the
gulls plummeted down towards the sea
once more.

Then her magical pony was turning away from Thrushcross harbour and flying away from the land, scanning the wide sea. There were grey ships on the horizon, gliding silently on their long journeys between continents, but no sign of Pale Moon. He turned back towards the land.

"Let's try along the shore," Krista suggested, thinking that the current might have swept Pale Moon into one of the tiny bays or inlets that ran as far as the eye could see.

So they flew on, low over the rocky shore, seeing only driftwood and wreckage from the flood – planks and car tyres, pieces of rope, plastic sacks, foam cushions.

"What a mess!" Krista sighed. She asked

Pale Moon

Star to fly more slowly, finding it hard to see deep into the dark clefts of rock.

They searched on. With every beat of Shining Star's strong wings, Krista felt hope slip away.

Then, around a distant headland, a boat chugged into view. Figures in bright orange jackets manned it – lifeboat men from a nearby port who had set out at dawn to find survivors.

Krista took a deep breath and crouched beneath Shining Star's wings as if to hide from the sailors. Then she remembered that the men couldn't see the beautiful white pony flying above their heads. It was part of his magic that he could surround himself with mist and disappear from view.

A sharp lookout might see that the small cloud drifting overhead was tinged with silver and dropping sparkling dust into the sea, but today everyone was too busy to notice.

"Thank heavens!" Krista murmured as the stout boat chugged on through the waves.

"Keep looking for Pale Moon!" Star urged.

He flew on, sometimes dangerously close to the cliffs as they searched the narrow coves. Waves crashed against the rocks, spraying white foam high into the air. The water sucked at the pebbles on the shore, tumbling over them in the rush to return to the sea.

"Slower!" Krista begged Star a second time. "It's so dark between the rocks that I can't see. I think there are caves where Pale Moon

120

might be sheltering. But I can't be sure."

Shining Star did his best to hover over each new cove. He scarcely beat his wings so that Krista could get a better look. First one, and then another – narrow cracks in the black rock with just enough space for him to fly.

"Yes, there's a cave!" Krista cried. She looked beyond the debris on the shore, into a dark, dry patch of pebbles beyond the reach of the waves. "You have to land and let me take a look!"

Star agreed. Carefully he lowered himself on to the tiny beach and waited for Krista to slip from his back. As soon as she felt her feet touch the pebbles, she began to run towards the narrow cave, calling out Pale Moon's name.

Pale Moon – moon – moon! An echo returned from the depths of the cave.

Startled, Krista stooped and entered, amazed to find that the rock opened out into a huge underground space, dry and warm.

The floor was strewn with heaps of dry seaweed and old driftwood – it was the perfect place to take shelter from the storm of the night before.

Pale Moon

"Pale Moon!" Krista called again.

Once more the echo returned.

She listened for a reply, searching deeper into the cave, but with faltering steps. "It's dark!" she called over her shoulder to Star.

Dark – dark – dark!

Krista stumbled against a rock. "There's no one here!"

Here – here!

With heavy steps she returned to the beach. "No," she reported with a shake of her head. Sadly she climbed back on to Star's back and they flew on with the diving gulls.

Three times Shining Star landed and three times Krista ran to search the dry caves lining the shore, squeezing through spaces

where the pony could not follow. Each cave was empty, except for the driftwood, plastic containers and frayed rope thrown up by the sea and lodged in crevices long ago.

"What now?" Krista sighed, wearily climbing on to Shining Star's back.

"We go on," he insisted firmly.

They came to another cave, even darker than before. "Perhaps!" Star murmured, landing gently on the tiny beach.

Krista glanced at his wise face. He seemed to be listening, his ears pricked towards the entrance to the cave. "Wait here," she told him, sliding to the ground and wearily approaching the entrance.

The walls of this cave were dripping wet.

124

Pale Moon

Krista looked up and saw a clear stream running down the hillside and over the entrance. There were green plants growing from the crevices in the rock, and moss everywhere. The walls of the cave were slimy with weeds. "I don't think Pale Moon will be in here!" she called back to Star.

"Look further!" he told her.

Ducking her head to avoid the low roof, Krista crept forward. "Pale Moon!" she called.

The echo came back, muffled by the sound of splashing water. Outside, in the open, Shining Star was distracted by the sound of an engine out to sea and the sight of the lifeboat trawling slowly along the shore.

Krista shook her head. There was no one here. She walked back towards Star. Then she stopped. Was that a sigh, coming from the depths of the cave?

No, it was water dripping from the roof, or a gust of wind blowing in from the sea.

Krista's feet crunched on.

"... My brother!" a voice whispered.

She stopped again. "Pale Moon?" she called softly.

Moon – moon!

"Shining Star, come quick!" This time Krista was sure she'd heard the voice. She turned back to face the darkness. "Pale Moon, where are you?" she called.

"Here!" said the whisper.

126

Pale Moon

Krista ran blindly in the direction of the voice, stumbling and falling, picking herself up and trying again. "Where? Talk to me! Tell me where you are!"

"Here!"

Here – here – here!

The echo filled the cave. Krista turned this way and that.

Then she saw a faint silver glow coming from behind a rock. She stumbled towards it, gasping when she reached the poor creature lying there on the wet ground.

Pale Moon looked up at Krista, scarcely able to lift her head. Her breath was shallow, her brown eyes almost closed.

Krista fell to her knees and reached out

a hand to stroke the magical pony's neck. "What happened?" she cried.

"I am very sick," Pale Moon told her, trying to stretch her tattered wings. She gave off a dim light that seemed to grow fainter by the second. "The water was strong, I was battered by the waves and dragged beneath the sea."

"But you're alive!" Krista said, stroking the pony then quickly taking off her jacket to lay it over Pale Moon. "And your brother is here to help you!"

"Call him!" the weak pony begged. There was a tear in her eye and her voice was almost too low for Krista to hear. "I wish to speak with him one last time!"

Chapter Nine

Krista ran to fetch Shining Star. "I've found her!" she cried. "But she's very weak. She wants to talk to you!"

The magical pony lowered his head to enter the cave. He followed Krista to the dark corner where his sister rested.

Pale Moon lay as before – her head against a rock, her wings folded against her shivering body. She looked up at Shining Star. "You came to help me," she murmured, "but I fear it is too late."

Star bent his neck to put his face close to hers,

breathing silver mist over her. "The wild ponies are safe," he told her.

Pale Moon closed her eyes and sighed. "That is good."

"Can you raise your head?" he asked.

His sister tried but was so weak that she sank back against the rock. "All my strength is gone," she whispered. "The water was stronger than me. My magic was powerless against the surge of the flood and the pull of the tide. It was only good fortune that tossed me through the waves to this place."

"And by good fortune we found you," Star replied.

Pale Moon sighed again. The glimmer of silver light that surrounded her was soft

130

and hazy. "Speak with our father when you return to Galishe. Say that his daughter bade him farewell before she went to the land of the spirits."

Tears came to Krista's eyes. She knelt beside Pale Moon, lifting the tangled mane clear of her face, softly stroking her head.

"Please stay with us! If you rest you'll get your strength back and we can lead you out of here!"

"Think of Galishe," Shining Star said softly. "Our father and our brother, North Star, wait eagerly for you to return to the meadow of white flowers and grass, where the water runs like sparkling diamonds."

"Galishe!" Pale Moon echoed, lifting her head from the rock. She seemed to be gazing into the far distance, imagining her perfect world.

But the world outside the cave broke in on her vision. The waves crashing against the shore grew louder and spray showered the narrow entrance.

Pale Moon

"The tide has turned!" Star told Krista.
"We must leave here before the sea returns!"

"Not without Pale Moon!" Krista cried. She
crouched over the weary, defeated pony. "Please,
you have to stand up. Then we can help you!"

Pale Moon struggled to tuck her legs under
her and push herself up from the ground.
But she was still too weak. "How will I ever fly
away from here?" she murmured, falling back
on to the rock.

"I'll bring water!" Krista promised. "Water
will help!" She dashed to the mouth of the
cave where she found a blue plastic container
amongst the debris. Remembering the trickling
stream of fresh water, she began to scale
the cliff, leaning out to fill the container.

133

Then she ran back to join Shining Star and
Pale Moon.

"Drink and you will gather strength," Star
promised. "Your wings will beat again, you
will rise into the air."

Outside, the waves broke and crashed on
to the shore, inching nearer.

Krista cupped her hand and poured water
into her palm. She offered it to Pale Moon,
who drank slowly.

Star nudged his sister with his nose.
"Soon you will fly with me into the skies,"
he told her. "We will be among the stars, you
and I. We will return home!"

Pale Moon nodded. She drank again. Then
she tried to stand.

Pale Moon

"You can do it!" Krista whispered, hearing the roar and rush of the waves outside.

The silver glow surrounding Pale Moon brightened a little as she struggled to her feet. She stood trembling, looking towards the light.

"Take a step!" Krista urged.

Pale Moon gathered her strength. She breathed a faint cloud of silver dust that fell on to the dark rock. Then she stepped forward.

"Oh!" Krista's heart lifted. "She's going to do it, just watch!"

One step and then another, then a pause to drink more water and listen to the encouraging words of Krista and Shining Star.

135

"We must hurry to beat the tide," Star whispered to Krista.

"Think of home!" Krista said to Pale Moon. "Think of flying through the night sky!"

So Pale Moon reached the mouth of the cave, where the brown water surged towards them. She faltered and turned to her brother.

"Come," he said, walking ahead of her and asking Krista to climb on to his back. The water swirled around her ankles as she stepped out to join him.

Slowly Pale Moon followed. As Shining Star spread his broad wings and shook silver from his feathers, she copied him.

"She's growing brighter!" Krista whispered. "She's coming back to life."

Pale Moon

"I will be by your side," he promised his
sister.

A wave broke and tugged at their feet, the
sound of the sea filled their ears.

Pale Moon's wings showered
silver dust on to the
water. She beat them
slowly, gazing
up towards the
clear sky.

"Good!" Star
whispered. He
and Krista
rose steadily
above the
ground.

Pale Moon looked up. She craned her neck towards them, beat her wings more strongly then lifted herself above the waves.

"Wonderful!" Krista whispered.

Shining Star beat his wings then soared on a current of air. Pale Moon rose in a silver mist, away from danger. She trailed magic dust through the morning air as she, Shining Star and Krista flew away.

They flew over Thrushcross, where the flood water was at last going down, and over the rocky ridge in time to see a woman in a Land Rover driving up from the valley to be reunited with her dog, Ben. The spaniel ran towards her and leaped with joy into her arms.

Behind him the small group of shaggy wild ponies made their way slowly down the hillside.

"All is well," Shining Star said quietly.

The words sank in. Krista took a deep breath and suddenly felt very tired. Her eyelids drooped and her whole body ached for clean sheets and a warm bed. "Take me home," she murmured in Star's ear.

He waited for Pale Moon to fly alongside him. "Come with us to Whitton," he said. "Krista must sleep."

His sister nodded, her eyes bright, the breeze lifting her mane from her beautiful face. She soared with him high into the sky and they entered a swirl of mist which became a glistening tunnel of wind and cloud,

whirling madly around them as they travelled through space and time.

Krista leaned sleepily against Shining Star's neck. *Safe!* she thought. *Everyone is safe!*

The sky was dark at the end of the tunnel. Stars twinkled. A bright moon shone.

Pale Moon flew silently beside Shining Star and Krista. They looked down on a quiet country where people slept and the embers of bonfires glowed red on the hillsides.

"Remember, remember the fifth of November!" Krista murmured dreamily.

They were back where they had started – flying over Whitton Bay towards High Point Farm where Krista's mum and dad were sound asleep.

Pale Moon

Star and Pale Moon landed quietly beside the house.

Krista slid from Star's back. Putting her arms around his neck, she hugged him hard.

"Go now," he whispered, a tear of joy in his eye.

Krista turned and stroked Pale Moon's face. "Star never lost hope," she told her. "He said, hope gets you a long way when there's danger around."

141

My Magical Pony

Pale Moon nodded. "He is a good brother. And I must thank you too, Krista, for all you have done to save my life."

Krista smiled happily. She stood back and watched the two magical ponies spread their wings. Soon they were above the roof, above the trees, flying in a cloud of silver, home to Galishe.

She crept into the silent house and looked out of the window. The ponies were gone, only the moon shone silver in their place.

Then, suddenly, a late firework shot into the dark sky. It whistled then exploded with a bang, showering red and gold sparks on to the earth, fading as they fell.

142

Pale Moon

Krista smiled, recalled meteors exploding around her and stars shooting through space. Then she climbed upstairs to bed.